WHOOPI GOLDBERG

Sugar Plum Ballerinas

Sugar Plums to the Rescue!

Sugar Plum Ballerinas

WHOOPI GOLDBERG

Sugar Plum Ballerinas

Sugar Plums to the Rescue!

with Deborah Underwood
Illustrated by Maryn Roos

 JUMP AT THE SUN BOOKS
New York

*This book is dedicated to ALL the fans of
the Sugar Plum Ballerinas who have a dream.*

Text copyright © 2011 by Whoopi Goldberg
Illustrations © 2011 by Maryn Roos

First Edition
1 3 5 7 9 10 8 6 4 2
V567-9638-5-11046

Printed in the United States of America

This book is set in 13 pt. Baskerville BT.
Reinforced binding

ISBN 978-1-4231-2083-4 (hardcover)
ISBN 978-0-7868-5264-2 (paperback)

Visit sugarplumballerinas.com,
www.jumpatthesun.com, and
www.disneyhyperionbooks.com

THIS LABEL APPLIES TO TEXT STOCK

Chapter 1

"Jessica, hurry! We're going to be late for class!"

Jerzey Mae peeks in through my doorway, her eyebrows knitted together with worry.

I look at my clock. "It's okay, Jerzey Mae. We have plenty of time," I say, in my best calm-Jerzey-Mae-down voice. I use it a lot, because she is always worrying. Ever since our little brother, Mason, helped her learn how to dance better, she's been a little more relaxed about things. But "a little more relaxed" for Jerzey Mae is about the same as "pretty freaked out" for most people.

Jerzey Mae bounces up and down on her toes for a moment, as if she has to go to the

1

bathroom, then tears down the hall. I hear her trying to rush our sister, JoAnn. Then I hear JoAnn replying, "Jerz! Relax! We don't have to leave for ten minutes!"

I grimace. Telling Jerzey Mae to relax is about the worst thing you can do. It usually makes her mad, which gets her even more wound up. But instead of howls, I hear the squeaking of floorboards and the creaking of springs as she walks back into her room and plops onto her bed to wait. Wow. She really has gotten better.

Time to feed my animals. I got my first pet, Herman the iguana, for my eighth birthday last year. I slip beet greens and part of a sweet potato into his cage. Walt the box turtle gets grated carrots and spinach. Shakespeare the rat scampers over and starts chomping on the lettuce I give him. I want to be a veterinarian or a poet when I grow up, but with all the food-preparation experience I'm getting, I could be a chef.

"Bar car far jar!" Edgar the mynah bird calls out as I put some banana slices into his food dish. I named him Edgar after Edgar Allan Poe, because Poe wrote a poem about a raven. I know a mynah bird isn't exactly a raven, but Mom and Dad said a raven wouldn't make a suitable pet. (Dad sometimes says Edgar isn't that suitable, either. Once, Mason left Edgar's cage open, and Dad woke up in the middle

of the night to find Edgar sitting on his chest reciting rhyming words. One of the words was *bed*, which I thought was very clever; but Dad wasn't impressed. I heard him scream from all the way in my bedroom.)

After everyone's been fed and I've double-checked that all the cages are closed, I look to see if I still have time left to read a little of my bird book. It's really interesting, and Edgar likes to look at the pictures with me. But now it really is time to get ready for class.

I change into my leotard and tights and put on my sneakers. Mom calls, "Girls! Time to go!" just as I toss my ballet slippers into my bag.

As I step into the hallway, Jerzey Mae bolts out of her room, nearly crashing into me. "Just a second," JoAnn drawls as we pass her bedroom door. She's slumped back in her chair playing a video skateboard game, with her baseball cap on backward, as usual. My parents aren't crazy about video games. But when JoAnn broke her leg last November, she was so miserable about not being able to do sports that they gave in and bought her some games so she could at least pretend to skateboard and play baseball.

It's weird how JoAnn, Jerzey Mae, and I are triplets—we don't look alike or act alike at all. Jerzey Mae is always buzzing around, running on nervous energy, and her wardrobe looks like a frilly Pepto-Bismol explosion: nothing but pink, pink, pink. JoAnn is a total tomboy, always wearing jeans and T-shirts. She moves slowly, unless she's on the soccer field or running the bases at a baseball game. And me? I'm in the middle. I'm not as skinny as Jerzey Mae or as muscle-y as JoAnn. Plus, I move at normal speed.

JoAnn peels herself off her chair and stands up in slow motion. "I'm coming, I'm coming," she says, seeing Jerzey Mae's panicked expression.

Mom meets us at the bottom of the stairs. Dad usually takes us to class on Saturdays, but he's out of the country for a month. He teaches African studies at a university, and he and another professor have taken a bunch of students to Botswana, where my grandfather came from. The house seems empty without Dad sitting in his study reading. And today it's especially quiet, since Mason is spending the weekend with one of his friends.

"All set, girls?" Mom asks. She usually dresses in suits—mom's a lawyer—but since it's the weekend, she's wearing jeans and a bright red coat. She looks us over: Jerzey Mae in her pink jacket, me in my brown coat, and JoAnn in a flimsy sweatshirt. "JoAnn, you're going to freeze. It's cold out there!"

JoAnn starts to roll her eyes, but Mom is not fond of eye-rolling, so JoAnn stops herself midroll. "I'll be fine."

"JoAnn . . ." Mom says.

6

"I'm going, I'm going." JoAnn sighs and heads upstairs.

"Careful of that leg!" Mom calls after her. JoAnn just got her cast off a few weeks ago, and the doctor told her to take it easy. "You're going to put yourself back in that hospital!"

This time I bet JoAnn *does* roll her eyes.

Chapter 2

I'm not crazy about New York in March. It's okay before Christmas, when there are decorations in the store windows and sparkling lights reflected in the snow. But afterward, it's pretty bleak until spring comes around. The trees are bare for the most part, and there's no snow right now—just a coating of ice on the sidewalk, which makes it hard to walk.

Jerzey Mae scurries ahead of us. Mom grips JoAnn's elbow tightly, in an attempt to keep her from slipping and breaking her other leg. I bring up the rear, composing a poem in my head as we go: *Frozen trees, sheets of ice, blowing winds . . .* What rhymes with *ice*? "Mice"? "Rice"?

Dead leaves flutters in a tree just ahead of us. "I wonder what kind of bird that is," Mom says, stopping for a second despite Jerzey Mae's pained "hurry up!" expression.

I quietly walk closer to the tree, trying not to scare the bird that Mom has observed. It's a pretty shade of gray, and it has black spots on its wings. "I think it's a mourning dove," I say.

Mom turns to me. "How on earth did you know that?"

I shrug. "It was in the bird book I'm reading."

Jerzey Mae grabs Mom's hand—the one that's not permanently attached to JoAnn's arm—and drags her forward. We start walking again.

"I thought you were reading a snake book," Mom says.

"That was last week," JoAnn tells her. "You're behind the times, Mom."

We arrive and climb the steps to the

Nutcracker School of Ballet. Mom gives us each a kiss. "Now, remember, Epatha's sister will pick you up today. I'm going in to the office for a bit."

"You work too hard, Mom," JoAnn says. "You need to chill out."

Mom raises an eyebrow. "My working hard pays for things like your skateboard video game, young lady."

That shuts JoAnn up.

Mom leaves, and Jerzey Mae, JoAnn, and I walk into the waiting room. All our friends are there already. Brenda has her nose buried in a medical book, as usual. Epatha is twirling around in front of Al and Terrel, showing off her new leotard. The colors are so crazy I know she must have dyed it herself.

"You look like a quetzal," I tell her.

"*¿Qué?*" Epatha responds, not sure if she should be insulted. "What? I look like a *che*?" Epatha's dad is Italian and her mom is Puerto

Rican, so she often talks in English, Italian, and Spanish all at the same time.

"It's a bird with beautifully colored feathers," I explain.

"Oh." She smiles and tosses her hair. "That's okay, then." She twirls one more time. "An Epatha original. Pretty fabulous, *sí*?"

"Very dramatic," says Al. "My mom would be proud." Al's mom is a clothing designer, so Al definitely knows dramatic.

Brenda puts down her book and looks at JoAnn's leg. "Today that on dance to going you are?" Brenda talks backward sometimes— she thinks it will make her smarter—but we can all understand her just fine.

"The doctor said she shouldn't jump, but she can do some of the other stuff," Jerzey Mae says.

Our teacher, Ms. Debbé, appears in the doorway of the waiting room. Today she's wearing a peacock blue jacket over some

11

simple black pants and a black turtleneck. There's a matching blue gem on the front of her black turban. She taps her walking stick on the floor. "The class, it begins," she says. (Although, since she's from France, it comes out more like, "*Ze class, eet begins.*")

When we enter the studio itself, Ms. Debbé motions for us to sit on the floor. "So," she says. "Today we will talk about our next

dance show, which will be at the end of April."

Ms. Debbé's voice sounds higher than usual. I look closely at her. Her face and her shoulders seem tense. I glance at my friends, but they don't seem to have noticed.

"Since spring will be here soon, this class will do little dances about spring things. Flowers. Spring rains. Birds." Ms. Debbé relaxes a little as she talks.

"Maybe quetzals," Epatha whispers to me. "I can wear this!" Ms. Debbé turns toward Epatha, who stops talking immediately.

Ms. Debbé pulls a list from her jacket pocket and begins telling us who's going to be in which dance. A group of girls on the other side of the room will be daffodils. Tiara Girl and three other kids are going to be a spring thunderstorm.

Terrel laughs. Even though she and Tiara Girl (whose real name is April) have stopped being openly nasty to each other—because

Terrel's dad is dating April's aunt—Terrel is still not April's biggest fan. "April showers. How appropriate," she mutters. JoAnn laughs, and Al hisses at them to be quiet before they get in trouble.

Ms. Debbé looks at us. "I should split you girls up, perhaps," she says. Then she sighs. "However, you will all dance the Dance of Robins Returning in the Spring."

JoAnn does not look thrilled about being a robin. "Tweet, tweet," she says under her breath. "Well, I guess it's better than being a stupid daffodil."

"I think it'll be fun," I say. I decide I'll look for robins in my bird book tonight, to see if I can get any inside information about how they move.

Ms. Debbé taps her cane for attention again.

"Now—" She stops speaking. We all look at her expectantly.

She takes a breath. "I . . ." Her gaze drifts across the room. I turn around to look, but don't notice anything unusual. Ms. Debbé just stands there. The silence probably lasts only ten seconds, but it feels much longer. Then Ms. Debbé snaps out of it.

"To the barre. For pliés," she says, her voice again as strong as ever.

"What was *that* about?" Al whispers as we walk to the barre.

"No idea," I say.

Class is good, just as it usually is. But Ms. Debbé definitely seems off. She is the most graceful person on the planet. If I were writing a poem about her, I would say she moves like a willow tree in a summer breeze. But as we line up at the end of the room to practice our grand jetés, I notice her stumble and almost trip. Something is definitely up.

After class is dismissed, my friends troop downstairs. "I'll be down in a minute," I call after them. They'll probably assume I'm going to the bathroom across the hall from the studio—but I'm not.

Ms. Debbé's office door is open just a crack. Inside, I see flashes of blue. She must be pacing back and forth.

I hesitate. I'm just a kid. Maybe Ms. Debbé doesn't want a kid sticking her nose into her business. But then I hear a strange, soft noise coming from the office. It sounds as if Ms. Debbé might be crying. Before I realize what I'm doing, I knock gently on the door.

A few seconds later, Ms. Debbé comes to the door. "Jessica!" she says, surprised. "I thought you left with your sisters."

"They're downstairs," I say. "I just . . . well, I wondered if you're okay. It seems like something's bothering you."

Ms. Debbé's face becomes rigid. "What makes you say that?" she asks.

I hadn't expected her to get mad at me.

"Uh . . . nothing," I reply, backing away from the door. "Just a feeling, I guess."

All of a sudden she looks resigned, as if she's given up trying to hide it. "You are a very observant child," she says. "Come in."

I step into her office. It's as elegant as she is, with a beautiful wooden desk, a chandelier, and a big, gold-framed mirror hanging on the wall.

Ms. Debbé picks up a piece of paper from her desk. "I just received this letter. You may have heard me speak of Mrs. Evans?"

I nod. Mrs. Evans is the old woman who owns the ballet school building. She comes to our dance shows sometimes.

"She passed away two days ago. She was an old friend, so that is sad for me."

"I'm really sorry," I say. Mrs. Evans seemed like a nice woman. She always wore interesting hats with feathers decorating them. "So . . . who owns the building now?"

17

"Mrs. Evans's son," Ms. Debbé says. She sighs.

I stand there quietly, trying to figure out what this might mean. "But the Nutcracker School can still stay here, right?" I finally ask.

She lifts an eyebrow. "I have a lease. Do you know what a lease is?"

Since Mom is a lawyer, I do; she talks about leases a lot. "It's an agreement between you and the person you rent from. It says how much rent you pay and stuff."

She nods. "The same lease *should* stay in place."

"Should?" I ask.

Ms. Debbé shrugs. "With these things, one never knows. Her son might find a way to raise the rent to something I cannot afford. Or, he might try to make the school leave altogether. It would be impossible to find another space like this. Mrs. Evans was very kind to the Nutcracker School. She loved the ballet, and she charged me less rent than she could have. Much less. I am afraid her son may not be so generous with us."

Suddenly, she shakes her head. "I think perhaps I am worrying too much, my dear. Forgive me. And please do not say anything to your friends. I am sure things will work out. They always seem to, thank goodness."

I nod, not sure if I'm supposed to go or not.

She smiles. "You should go, Jessica. I am sure your sisters are waiting for you. But thank you for noticing my sadness. You are a very sensitive girl."

She seems to be feeling better. But as I walk down the stairs, I'm definitely feeling worse.

Chapter 3

"What took you so long?" JoAnn says, as I join her, Jerzey Mae, Epatha, and Epatha's older sister, Amarah, in the waiting room. "Did you fall into the toilet?"

I ignore her and quickly put on my sneakers and coat.

"Let's go," Amarah says. She's in college, so she's really a grown-up, but she's funny, and being with her doesn't feel like being with a parent.

It's started to snow, and Epatha runs around trying to catch snowflakes on her tongue. The others walk together, talking and laughing.

I follow behind, my head spinning. I wonder if the Nutcracker School really is in danger. It's the only place I can count on seeing all my friends, since we don't go to the same school. If it weren't for ballet class, we would never even have met. We wouldn't be the Sugar Plum Sisters.

A tiny mewing sound interupts my thoughts. I stop to try to see where it's coming from. There's not much around—just a Dumpster pushed up against the side of a brick apartment building.

By now my friends are quite a ways ahead of me. "Come on, Jessica!" JoAnn hollers.

"Just a second," I yell back, hearing something mew again. It sounds as if it's coming from under the Dumpster. I do a grand plié—who knew ballet would be useful in real life?—and peer underneath.

Two glowing amber eyes peer back at me.

"You guys!" I shout. "Come here!"

I reach under the Dumpster and scoop out a kitten, which isn't easy, since I'm wearing gloves. The kitten howls in protest.

The other girls run back and gather around.

"Oooh, let me see!" Epatha leans over so her face is two inches from the kitten's.

"Don't get so close, Epatha!" says JoAnn as she pulls her back. "You'll freak him out."

The kitten is almost all black, but has little white boots on each foot and a white mark on his head. He's so skinny I can see his ribs sticking out from under his fur. After strug-

gling for a moment to get away, he seems to give up. I can feel his heart pounding.

"Oh, he's so cute!" Jerzey Mae says.

"Maybe you should just put him back," Amarah says hesitantly. "His mother might still be around."

No way am I putting the kitten back in the snow. I can't do anything about Ms. Debbé's problem, but this is a small, kid-size problem I *can* do something about—a kitten in distress. "If he was being taken care of, do you think he'd be this skinny?" I ask.

Epatha reaches out to pet the kitten, but Amarah stops her. "Don't touch it—it might bite you or something."

"Jessica's touching it!" Epatha complains. "Why can't I?"

"She's wearing gloves. Like I am," Amarah says. She takes the kitten from me and examines it. "It looks like something's wrong with his front paw."

"Well, then, we have to do something about it," I say firmly.

JoAnn groans. "You're crazy, girl," she says. "You know we can't have a cat. Dad's totally allergic."

For once, I roll my eyes at her. "I *know*," I say. "But we can get his paw taken care of and take him somewhere safe, like an animal shelter." I look at the apartment buildings around the Dumpster. "I wonder what happened to his mother."

Amarah looks around. "Who knows? He looks like he's in pretty bad shape, though." She pauses to think. "My boyfriend's cousin Brian is a vet. I wonder . . . just a sec."

She hands the kitten back to me, takes out her phone, and walks away. I can feel the cat shivering even through my gloves. He must be freezing. "Don't worry, little guy," I say. "We'll take care of you."

"Jessica," JoAnn pleads.

"What?" I say. "We should just leave him here to freeze to death? No way."

"Okay." Amarah puts the phone back into her purse. "We can go to Brian's, and he'll check the kitten out. But Brian can't keep him," she says, before I can even ask. "You guys will have to figure out what to do with your little furry friend after that."

"Fine," I say.

"Fine?" JoAnn looks at me like I'm nuts. "Exactly how is that *fine*?"

"Fine," I say, in a louder voice.

So, we take a detour to the vet's apartment. I hold the kitten under my coat to try to keep him warm. Luckily, Brian doesn't live too far away. Also luckily, we were planning to hang out at *Bella Italia*, the restaurant Epatha's parents own, before Amarah took us home. This means that Rose, our housekeeper and sometime babysitter, won't wonder where we are and expect us back.

As Brian examines the kitty on his kitchen table, we gather around to watch.

"Hmmm . . . the kitten is definitely under-nourished. She's about four months old, I'd guess," he says.

"She?" Jerzey Mae asks.

He nods. "*That* I'm sure about." He pries open the kitten's mouth to check her teeth, then uses a shiny, cylinder-shaped instrument to peer into her ears.

We stand lined up against the kitchen

wall as he continues his examination. JoAnn is unusually worked up, shifting her weight from side to side impatiently. "Jessica," she hisses, "what are we gonna do with that cat?"

I'm worrying about the same thing. There was no way I was going to leave him— her—out in the cold with an injured paw. But what *are* we going to do with her?

JoAnn continues, "You can't just hide her in your room, you know."

"That's it!" I say. "Dad won't be back for a few more weeks. That'll give us time to find the kitten a home. Mom won't even have to know."

JoAnn shakes her head vigorously. "Oh, no. You're crazy. And I am *not* going to help. And neither is Jerzey Mae."

"Help what?" Jerzey Mae says, hearing her name.

"How's the patient?" Epatha asks loudly, sensing a storm brewing.

27

Brian puts away his stethoscope. "She's in remarkably good health, considering. Her paw is bleeding, but it's not too serious. She may have just cut herself on some glass or a bit of metal. I'll bandage it up, but she'll be fine in no time."

We're silent as we watch him wrap the paw in a little bandage. The kitten seems too overwhelmed by everything to protest, although every once in a while she lets out a pitiful, tiny meow. But then the vet gives her a little bit of cat food, which she gobbles up in a flash.

"There you are!" Brian says, handing her to me. "I'd recommend you take her in for a more thorough checkup and blood work, and make sure you get her her vaccination shots. But it looks like you girls have a lovely new pet."

"Fabulous," JoAnn says unenthusiastically.

Brian also warns us to feed her only a little bit at a time, so she doesn't make herself sick.

He loans us a cat carrier for the trip home. After the kitten is inside, we thank him and head out into the cold.

Amarah stops and turns around to face us. "You know this cat has to live somewhere," she says.

Epatha looks at her. "Hey! Maybe we can keep—"

"No way," Amarah says. "You know Nonna thinks cats are bad luck."

Epatha lives with her mom, dad, *and* two grandmas. One of her grandmas is very superstitious. She's always tossing salt over her shoulder or making spitting noises to scare away evil spirits.

I think fast. Mom won't be home yet. And Jerzey Mae and JoAnn can distract Rose while I get the carrier upstairs.

But then what?

"Sugar Plum emergency meeting," I say. "Now."

29

Chapter 4

As we walk, Epatha borrows Amarah's phone and calls Terrel, who is our best organizer, even though she's a year younger than we are. Terrel says she'll call Brenda and Al. And Jerzey Mae calls Rose and asks if it's okay for us to have a few friends over.

"Why don't we just take her to the shelter?" Amarah asks.

"Because," I say, "we want to make sure it's a good shelter. Some shelters kill the animals if they don't get adopted. And no one"— I look at her fiercely—"is killing this cat."

The good thing about being calm most of the time is that when you're *not* calm, people don't argue with you.

"Fine," Amarah says, although she still looks uncertain. She drops us off at our front door and says she'll be back later to get Epatha.

"Okay—what's the plan?" I ask. "We need to sneak her into the house."

"You don't have a plan?" Jerzey Mae squeaks. "I thought you had a plan!"

"Well, I said I'm not helping," JoAnn says. "Jessica's nuts."

"I'll help," Epatha says, pushing past JoAnn. "You want distraction? I'll give you distraction."

She rings the doorbell. Rose answers.

"Hello, girls," she says. "What are you doing out—"

"Oh, my *gosh*!" Epatha yells, pushing past her. "I *totally* have to go to the bathroom. Now! Rose! Help! Where is it? You have one downstairs, don't you?" She hops up and down on one foot and careens into the wall, almost knocking one of Dad's African masks to the floor.

Rose leaps for the mask and catches it just in time. "This way! This way!" she says, dashing ahead of Epatha (who knows very well where the downstairs bathroom is).

"Wow!" JoAnn says.

"Come on!" I say, running upstairs while trying not to jostle the kitten too much in the carrier.

We make it to my room, then slam the door shut. JoAnn also closes the door that connects my room to Jerzey Mae's.

"Good idea," I tell JoAnn. "I've read that you should keep a new cat in one part of the house so she doesn't get too scared."

"Actually," JoAnn says, "I think we should keep her in one part of the house so she doesn't use my skateboard as a scratching pad. Or go to the bathroom on Jerzey Mae's comforter."

Jerzey Mae's eyes widen in horror. "She wouldn't do that, would she?"

Jerzey Mae loves that pink, fluffy comforter. Thanks a lot, JoAnn, I think.

"Of course not," I say. "Cats are very good about using litter boxes." As I say this, however, I realize that we do not *have* a litter box.

Just then, the doorbell rings, and we hear footsteps pounding up the stairs. I open my door a crack. Terrel, Brenda, and Al are waiting in the hallway. "Come in as fast as you can," I say.

Terrel hurries through the door carrying a bag of cat litter that she has smuggled in under her coat. Al has a shallow aluminum pan that will work just fine as a litter box for a little cat. And as they sit down, Brenda pulls several cans of cat food out of her backpack, as well as a little cat dish.

Relief floods through my body. "How did you know we'd need this stuff?" I ask.

"Because I'm *good*," Terrel responds, opening the litter and dumping it into the pan. "Now. Where's this cat?"

The kitten is huddled in the carrier. Having three more people clambering around has clearly made her even more nervous. Even when I open the door, she stays put.

"Here, kitty, kitty, kitty," says Al, getting down on her knees to peer inside.

"I'll bet she comes out in a minute," I say. "Let's just be quiet and see."

Sure enough, as soon as we all stop talking and moving around, a tiny white paw emerges from the carrier. The kitten slowly comes out, then sits and stares at each one of us. It looks as if she's called this meeting and is about to give a speech.

"Oh, she's so cute!" Al whispers. "What's her name?"

"I don't know yet," I say.

"And look at that mark on her head,"

Terrel says. "It reminds me of something."

"Ms. Debbé's turban!" Brenda says.

"That's it!" Terrel says. "You should name her Adrienne—that's Ms. Debbé's first name, right?"

I nod and consider this. That mark *does* look like a turban, and cats are elegant and graceful, just like Ms. Debbé.

"Adrienne it is," I declare.

Adrienne tentatively steps forward. I

gently scoop her up and put her in my lap. She bounds off me immediately, then sits on the floor and starts licking her back leg.

"Not a lap cat, I guess," says Epatha.

"Give her some food," Terrel commands.

I open a container of food and put a tiny bit in front of Adrienne. She wolfs it down in just a few seconds. Then she starts enthusiastically washing her face with her paw.

"Oh, I wish I could have a cat," Brenda says.

I look at her hopefully, but she shakes her head. "Nope. No pets. It's in our lease."

"Ours, too," Al says sadly.

We all look at Terrel.

"Nope," Terrel responds. "Dad says our place is full enough with all the kids."

Terrel has four older brothers living with her and their dad, so I guess her dad has a point.

"So, what do I do?" I say. My voice rises.

I'm not a panicky person, but I suddenly realize I'm in kind of a mess here.

"Shelters," Terrel says. "We'll each call some."

The other girls nod.

Right. Surely, this isn't the first cat in New York that ever needed to find a home. "But we have to find a really good one. One that doesn't kill the animals," I say.

It dawns on me that if something goes wrong and we end up having to put Adrienne in a shelter that *does* kill animals, it will be all my fault. My eyes start to fill with tears. What have I done? Maybe I should have left her out on the street.

Al puts her arm around me. "Of course. Don't worry. This'll be a piece of cake."

I sure hope she's right.

Chapter 5

I look up animal shelters online, and each of my friends leaves with a list of places to call. JoAnn surprises me by offering to make the first bunch of calls, even though she hates talking on the phone.

"I think maybe she likes you after all," I whisper to Adrienne.

Meanwhile, Jerzey Mae and I play with Adrienne. Terrel, the genius, even thought to bring over a few cat toys—she got them from her neighbor, who runs a pet store—and so we dangle a furry mouse in front of Adrienne and watch her pounce. Shakespeare the rat is up high enough that he can't see the kitten playing on the floor, which is probably a good thing. Herman the iguana and Walt the box turtle don't seem to mind. But Edgar doesn't seem too happy about the new addition. "Bat cat mat!" he screeches.

"*Shhhhh!*" Jerzey Mae says. "How does he know Adrienne is a cat?"

"He doesn't," I say. "You know he just says strings of words. I guess he got lucky." Still, it's not going to help me keep Adrienne hidden if Edgar's screaming about cats at the top of his lungs. I cover up his cage and he quiets down.

JoAnn comes back in holding the phone and her list of shelters. "Sheesh," she says. "These shelters are all crazy," she says, slumping onto the floor and leaning back against my bed.

"What do you mean?" I ask.

She shakes her head and looks at the list. "One place only takes dogs. One only takes a certain *kind* of dog. One only takes reptiles. And two only take animals after they come in for an examination and blood tests; and neither of those has any appointments for a month."

"A month!?" I say. How can we possibly hide Adrienne in my room for that long? All of a sudden I can't breathe. My heart pounds even harder in my chest.

"Relax," JoAnn says, a little alarmed at my panicked reaction. "We're all calling places, remember? Something will turn up."

But it doesn't.

By late that afternoon, the other Sugar Plums have all reported back. They haven't had any luck, either. It's the same story everywhere: too many animals, not enough room. And the places that sound like they're good want to do an exam first, but don't have any appointments for weeks.

"Why are there so many cats?" Terrel yells over the phone.

"Because people don't get their cats neutered or spayed," I tell her.

"Get them *what*?" she asks.

"Those are operations that prevent the cats from having babies," I say. "If they're not spayed or neutered, the cats have lots of kittens; then there are too many cats around. So people end up killing them."

Terrel is silent for a minute. "That's awful. You'd better get Adrienne spayed," she says.

I tell her the shelter will take care of that— if we ever get Adrienne *into* a shelter, that is.

We finally take the first appointment we can find. It's going to be at the Cat Crazy Animal Shelter in Brooklyn. JoAnn helps me look up reviews of the shelter online to make sure people like it, and, thank goodness, they do. Unfortunately, our appointment is three weeks away. But at least the timing works out so that Adrienne will be in the shelter by the time Dad gets home—though just barely.

After we make the appointment, JoAnn, Jerzey Mae, and I sit in my room and stare silently at Adrienne, who is now curled up and asleep in a shoe box.

"At least she's quiet," Jerzey Mae observes. "My friend Kate had a cat that meowed his head off all the time."

She's right—Adrienne hasn't meowed at all since we brought her home.

JoAnn shakes her head. "I don't care how quiet she is. No way will you be able to keep her hidden from Mom and Rose for three weeks."

"Thanks for the vote of confidence," I say. "We don't have a choice! What else can we do with her?"

We're silent again for a minute. Then Jerzey Mae jumps to her feet. "How about ballet?" she says.

"Ballet?" I ask. "I don't think dancing will help right now, Jerzey Mae."

"That's not what I mean!" she says. "The ballet school is pretty big. Aren't there some rooms upstairs that no one uses? Maybe Ms. Debbé would let us keep Adrienne in one of them, at least for a little while."

JoAnn and I exchange a look. "That's actually not a bad idea," JoAnn says.

Jerzey Mae beams.

"But who'd feed her?" I ask. "And clean her litter box?"

"There are classes there every day," JoAnn says. "And Ms. Debbé's son, Mr. Lester, uses the rooms for rehearsals at night. Maybe he could help." Mr. Lester teaches at the school sometimes.

I can't imagine Ms. Debbé scooping out a litter box, but Mr. Lester seems more down to earth than his mom.

"Maybe," I say, a bubble of excitement growing inside me. "If we could just keep her there for a few weeks, that would be enough time to get her into a shelter. Or find her another home."

"But we can't ask Ms. Debbé till our next class. That's two days away," Jerzey Mae says. "What do we do until then? What about Rose coming in to clean?"

JoAnn sits bolt upright. "She's on vacation next week!" she says. "Remember? She's going to visit her sister."

"Right!" I say, jumping to my feet. "So, we'll just keep our doors closed and keep Mom away. And hope that Edgar stays quiet."

In response, Edgar makes a chattering noise.

"I don't think it's Edgar we need to worry about," says JoAnn.

Almost on cue, we hear the bouncing of a basketball out in the hallway. "Hey, I'm home! Are you guys here?"

JoAnn's right. We totally forgot about the one thing that could ruin our plan.

Mason.

Chapter 6

"Oh, no," breathes Jerzey Mae.

"Just a sec, Mason," JoAnn calls. "Do something!" she hisses to me, waving her arms around in the air.

The door rattles, sending Adrienne scurrying under the bed. "Let me in!" Mason calls. "I want to show you the cool frog book Tyrone's mom got me."

"You don't want to come in here right now," JoAnn says. "We're talking about girl stuff."

The basketball stops thumping. "What kind of girl stuff?" Mason asks through the door.

JoAnn looks around quickly, as though she's searching for an idea. "Bras!" she calls back. "We're talking about bras. Pink, frilly bras."

"*Ewww!*" Mason groans in disgust. "Girls are so gross. I am *out* of here." Mason starts dribbling the ball again, then clomps down the stairs.

"Nice," I say to JoAnn. "Thanks."

She nods. "Well, we've gotta think of a better reason to keep him out of here. He's not going to believe we're talking about bras for the next two days."

I pull Adrienne out from under the bed. I try putting her on my lap again, and again she jumps right off, although this time she curls up right beside me. "I suppose we could tell Mason about Adrienne."

"You've got to be kidding!" JoAnn says. "Remember when we were trying to keep Mom's birthday present a secret? He blabbed like five seconds after we told him."

I scratch Adrienne's chin. "That was a whole year ago," I say. "He's older now. What do you think, Jerzey Mae?"

She looks a little sick. "I think we're going to get in trouble. *Big* trouble," she says faintly.

Hiding Adrienne isn't as hard as I'd feared. On Sunday, Mom takes us all out to the zoo, so no one's home to hear Adrienne skittering around or pouncing on things. I also manage to keep Mason out of my room after school on Monday, by telling him Shakespeare's not feeling well and needs quiet. I feel bad about lying, but I don't know what else to do. I feel especially terrible when Mason quietly knocks on the door with a get-well card he made for Shakespeare, with drawings of all of his favorite foods on it. "That'll cheer him up," Mason says confidently. "Can I give it to him?"

I tell him Shakespeare's asleep. "But I'll give him the card as soon as he wakes up. I know he'll love it," I say quickly, seeing the disappointed look on Mason's face. I feel like a horrible sister. But with luck, by tomorrow our problems will be solved. If Mrs. Debbé says Adrienne can stay at the school, we'll run home and get the kitty and her things right away. Hopefully by tomorrow night, Adrienne will be settled in her new temporary home.

On Tuesday, JoAnn, Jerzey Mae, and I race home from school to get ready for ballet. Mason's at his own ballet class, thank goodness, so we don't have to worry about him snooping around. I make sure Adrienne's litter box is clean and give her another help-ing of some canned food. She meows happily this time as she digs in. I think she's gotten bigger just in the last few days. Her ribs don't seem to stick out quite as much. She must really have been starving before.

I carefully close my door, making sure it latches, and join JoAnn and Jerzey Mae on the stairway. When I get to the bottom, I realize I've forgotten something—a photo I took of the kitten. She's so cute that seeing the picture may convince Ms. Debbé to help her.

"Just a sec," I say. I run upstairs to my room, grab the picture, and close the door again.

Mason's door opens, and his head pops out into the hallway. "How's Shakespeare?" he asks.

Chapter 7

My heart stops. "What are you doing here?" My voice sounds high and squeaky. "You're supposed to be at ballet!"

"Nope," he says. "My ballet school is off this week."

I think I hear Adrienne mewing behind the door. I cough loudly to cover the sound. "But you can't stay home by yourself!" I say. I cough again.

"Are you sick?" Mason asks.

I shake my head wildly.

Mason continues. "Anyway, I'm not by myself. Rose just got here. Mom asked her to come in today so she can take care of me. Not that I need anyone to take care of me, since I'm almost eight," he says.

Oh, no. If Rose is around, either she or Mason could wander into my room. I start to panic. What am I going to do?

"Are you sure you're not sick, Jessica?" Mason asks. "You look funny."

Maybe I should pretend to be sick, so I can stay home. But then Rose would be in my room every five minutes, bringing me cinnamon toast and orange juice. There's only one thing to do.

"I'm fine," I say. "But I forgot something." Adrienne mews and I cough loudly again as I go back into my room and slam the door behind me.

"Sorry, kitty," I whisper as I scoop Adrienne up and put her into my dance bag. "I'm afraid you're coming to class."

I pick up the bag gingerly. Will she be okay in there? Luckily my bag is big, so I'm sure she'll have enough air. But I'm worried that she might get smooshed inside. So I take her out, put her into her favorite shoe box, and put the shoe box, without its lid, into the bag. At least that will keep the sides of the bag from collapsing around her. I toss some dried food into the box, hoping it will keep her from meowing. Then I zip up the bag and glide slowly out of my room, trying not to jostle her.

Mason is still standing there, watching. "Why are you walking funny?" he asks.

"I'm not," I say, carefully moving down the stairs.

"Jessica!" JoAnn yells.

"Coming!" I yell back.

Mom and the others are waiting for me by the door. "Hurry! Hurry!" Mom says, helping me put on my coat. She stops. "Jessica, is your bag rattling?"

Yes, it is. Adrienne must be playing with the bits of kibble in the shoe box. I cough again loudly to distract Mom.

"Are you okay?" Mom asks, concerned.

"Yes," I lie. But I'm not okay—my throat is getting sore from all this fake coughing. "We'd better hurry. You need to get back to work, right? Let's go!"

Jerzey Mae and JoAnn stare at me.

Mom checks her watch. "Yes, I do. Come on, girls." She opens the door for us, and we head out. I try to keep as much distance as I can between Mom and my bag.

Mom and Jerzey Mae walk ahead. JoAnn hangs back.

"What is up with you?" she asks us in a whisper.

As if in response, Adrienne mews loudly. JoAnn's eyes pop open wide. She looks down at my dance bag.

"Don't tell me that cat is in there!" she says.

"*Shhh!*" I say, walking a little more slowly

to let Mom and Jerzey Mae get even farther ahead.

"Jessica! Why in the world—"

"Because Mason's home!" I say, louder than I mean to. I'm already worried enough. I don't need my sister yelling at me on top of it. My voice drops back to a whisper. "*And* Rose. What was I going to do, lock Adrienne in my closet?"

As I say it, I realize that that wouldn't have been the worst idea in the world. Mason never goes in my closet, and Rose hardly ever does. Frankly, taking Adrienne to ballet was probably the worst idea in the world. But it's too late now.

JoAnn closes her eyes and shakes her head. "Well, don't tell Jerzey Mae. She'd probably pass out. And you'd better ask Ms. Debbé if the cat can stay at the school just as soon as we get there. We don't want a repeat of the rat incident."

Last year, Mason had to come to class with us, and during one visit he had the bright idea of bringing Shakespeare along. Shakespeare escaped in the ballet studio and ended up crawling into the handbag of Miss Camilla Freeman, a very famous ballerina who was visiting. Needless to say, this was not a good situation.

I nod in agreement. "I'll go to her office as soon as we get there," I tell JoAnn.

Mom walks us to the door of the Nutcracker School. "Have a good class," she says, as she kisses each one of us.

I race through the door and into the waiting room, leaving my sisters behind.

"Hey, Jessica," Epatha calls from our usual bench. Today she's dressed in a bright pink leotard, and has a gold spangly headband. Al stands nearby, her leg propped up on the bench to stretch.

"Oh, uh, hi," I say, peering through the

glass window that separates the waiting room from the ballet office. Sometimes, Ms. Debbé is in there before class, but not today.

Mr. Lester walks into the waiting room, along with Jerzey Mae and JoAnn. "Hello, girls," he says to us.

"Hey, Mr. Lester," Terrel says. "What are you doing here?" Mr. Lester hasn't been around much this year, because he's been busy with rehearsals at the Harlem Ballet.

"I'm teaching your class today," he says. "Ms. Debbé has a meeting."

"Oh, no!" I say, before I realize what I'm doing. Mr. Lester raises one eyebrow. "I mean, I just really wanted to talk to her about something," I add quickly.

Mr. Lester glances upstairs. "Well, she's up in her office now," he says. "The guy she's meeting with hasn't shown up yet. Maybe you could duck in really fast before he gets here."

"Okay," I say, relieved. I race up the stairs

as fast as I can. Adrienne doesn't seem to mind. In fact, she's been very quiet for the last few minutes.

All of a sudden, I'm worried. I hope she's okay. Maybe I have bumped her around more than I thought. I go into the bathroom, lock the door, and open the bag. Adrienne, thankfully, is curled up in the box. I see the side of her little body rise and then gently fall as she breathes in and out.

I start to zip the bag back up but stop when I hear a deep voice outside.

"Ms. Debbé?"

I open the bathroom door a crack. A tall man in a suit stands waiting at the door to Ms. Debbé's office. I hear Ms. Debbé say something in response, and then the man goes in to her office.

I creep out of the bathroom and into the hall.

"I know you're busy, so I'll get to the point,"

says the man, as he sits down in the chair across from Ms. Debbé's desk. The office door is not completely closed. "As you know, I now own this building. I have a developer interested in building condominiums here."

I get a sick feeling in my stomach. This must be the son of the nice landlady that Ms. Debbé was renting the building from.

The man continues. "That means, of course, that this building would need to be razed."

I frown. How would they *raise* a building? Do they mean they're building another floor on top or something?

Then it hits me. I remember Dad talking about an old building at the university where he teaches. He said the building needed to be "razed." But it didn't mean lifting the building up.

It meant tearing it down.

Chapter 8

My head is spinning. Tearing down the building would mean the end of the Nutcracker School. Ms. Debbé told me before that she could only afford the rent on this place because the old landlady, Mrs. Evans, was nice and gave her a good deal. I blink back tears as I think of losing this school, this place where my friends and I all come together.

Ms. Debbé's walking stick thumps on the floor. "Throwing me out of the building—you cannot do this. It is not legal." Her French accent gets thicker, as it always seems to when she is upset.

The man sighs. "Please understand. I don't want this to be a difficult process," he says.

"However, I need to demolish this building."

"But you can't—"

The man cuts Ms. Debbé off.

"I will compensate you for moving expenses. You need to be out in thirty days. The construction crew is already lined up, and they need to start work in April."

Ms. Debbé's voice becomes icy. "I am sorry you don't want this to be difficult. But it will be difficult, I can assure you. This lease"—I hear her rustling some papers in her hand—"it means something. It is a legal agreement."

The man's voice becomes harsh. "That lease is a very long document, as you know," he says. "If I can find any way that you've broken even one of the terms of the lease, I have the legal right to evict you. And surely you have broken the terms, if only in some small way. It will just be a matter of finding out how. And that will take time, time that I'd prefer not to spend."

It is silent for a moment. Then the man says, "All right. I'll give you moving expenses, as well as pay two months' rent on your new facility."

"There is no new facility!" Ms. Debbé says sharply. "If you do this, the school will close. And will I allow that to happen? No. I will not."

There's another brief silence. The man must be as surprised as I am at Ms. Debbé's having yelled like that. I imagine she's now glaring at him from across her desk. I would not want to be on the receiving end of one of her glares.

My left leg starts to feel as if it's fallen asleep. I shift my weight as slowly as I can from one leg to the other, but a floorboard creaks.

"Is someone out there?" Ms. Debbé asks.

I freeze, my heart pounding. Maybe I can make it to the stairs and run—but when I try to slide away, the floor creaks even more loudly.

"Hello? Who is there?" Ms. Debbé calls again.

Slowly, I peer around the door jamb. Ms. Debbé and the man both stare at me. "I . . . uh . . . I just wanted to talk to you about something," I say. "But it can wait," I add hastily. "I'll just go back down to . . ."

"No. You will not," Ms. Debbé says. "You are my student. This man"—she gives him a haughty look—"is not part of my ballet school. *He* can wait." She thumps her walking

stick emphatically on the floor.

All of a sudden my bag seems to yowl and wiggle. In a flash, Adrienne jumps out and races across the floor, tucking herself under the chest of drawers near Ms. Debbé's desk.

"What on earth?" Ms. Debbé's eyebrows shoot up in surprise.

"I'm sorry! I'm sorry!" I say, running over to the chest of drawers. I reach underneath to grab Adrienne, but she keeps scooting away.

Finally, I manage to pull her out; I drop her back into my bag and zip it up.

"Jessica, why would you do this thing?" Ms. Debbé asks. "A ballet school, it is not a place for a cat."

My cheeks feel hot. I look from Ms. Debbé to the man, who seems to be ignoring us as he flips through a stack of papers.

"I know. I'm sorry." My words come out in a rush. "It's just that we found her, and she needs a home, and we can't get her into a shelter for a few weeks, and we were wondering if maybe she could stay here in one of the rooms upstairs that nobody uses."

"Aha!" the man says, jumping to his feet.

Inside my bag, Adrienne meows loudly in response.

" 'Aha' what?" Ms. Debbé asks coldly.

The man smiles. "No animals 'are allowed to enter the building.' I just found it right here in the lease. Section 117a." He shakes the papers he's been rifling through.

I'm not sure exactly what this means, but I'm guessing it's not good.

Ms. Debbé stands very still, like a statue. Then she speaks. "Surely, this does not break the lease. I didn't even know the cat was here," she says. But her voice doesn't sound as strong as it did before.

The man holds the lease out to her and points to something on the page. "The only exceptions are for service animals." He turns to me. "I don't suppose that's a Seeing Eye cat you have there, little girl?"

I usually bristle at being called a little girl, but this doesn't seem like the time to argue about that. "No," I say.

He smiles and folds up the lease, then puts it into his briefcase. "Well, I guess that settles it," he says. "Thirty days." He stands up and moves toward the door. "It was a pleasure meeting you, Ms. Debbé."

Then he looks at me. "And thank you," he says. "You made this process much easier for everyone." He walks out the door.

I start to realize what has just happened. It's so horrible that it's taking some time to sink in. "Ms. Debbé," I whisper. "Did the cat make you lose your lease?"

She doesn't answer for a moment. Then she says, "That man was determined to make us leave, Jessica. If it hadn't been the cat, he would have found something else. I am sure of it."

In other words, *yes*.

My eyes fill with tears. "Ms. Debbé, I am so sorry," I say. "I never meant . . ."

She nods. "I know you didn't mean any harm, my dear. It was just . . . how do you say . . . a very unfortunate incident." Her face is stiff, as if what just occurred hasn't sunk in with her yet, either.

I sniff and wipe my eyes on my sleeve.

"What will happen to the school? Will it really have to close?"

Ms. Debbé leans back in her chair. It's the first time in my life I've ever seen her without 100 percent perfect posture. She looks much older than she usually does. And very, very sad.

"I will talk with a lawyer. Perhaps there is something that can be done," she says. But there's no hope in her voice.

Adrienne mews from inside the bag. "I guess this means the cat can't stay here," I say in a small voice.

Her eyes meet mine, and a hint of the old, fierce Ms. Debbé shines through. "No, Jessica, I think that under the circumstances, that would not be appropriate."

I nod and slink out of her office.

"What did she say?" JoAnn asks quietly as I rejoin the others in the waiting room. "Can the cat stay here?"

I shake my head. I don't say anything more, because I'm afraid I might start crying again.

JoAnn exhales heavily. "That's tough luck," she says.

Epatha, Terrel, and Al are bent over the anatomy book Brenda's reading. Brenda's probably showing them an interesting muscle or blood vessel. Jerzey Mae is hanging near the back, because looking at Brenda's books usually makes her sick to her stomach. The other girls in the waiting room are talking, stretching, and putting on their ballet slippers. Across the room, Tiara Girl brags about how she got to go to a very expensive Broadway musical last weekend.

For everyone else, it's just a normal day at the Nutcracker School of Ballet.

For me, it's the worst day of my life. Because now the school is going to close. And it's all my fault.

Chapter 9

Even though Ms. Debbé's meeting is over—
very over, thanks to me—Mr. Lester still
leads our class. He doesn't let on that he
knows anything, so maybe Ms. Debbé hasn't
told him the bad news yet.

The only good thing is that Adrienne has
gone back to sleep, and is snoozing quietly
in her shoe box. Not that she can cause any
more trouble than she already has.

But that's not fair. It's not her fault that
she jumped out of the box earlier. She was
just being a kitten. It's the fault of the stupid
kid who took her to ballet school in the first
place.

That would be me.

In class, we do pliés, tendus, grand jetés, chaîné turns, and all the usual ballet stuff, but it's as if I'm not even really there. I keep banging into people and turning in the wrong direction, just as Jerzey Mae used to before Mason taught her how to do ballet better. JoAnn even calls me Jerzey Mae as a joke. The real Jerzey Mae overhears this and gives JoAnn a hurt look.

I'm not used to thinking about two huge problems at the same time—the ballet school's fate, the kitten—it all seems so hopeless. I do a chaîné turn and crash into Terrel.

"Holy cow," she mutters. "What is up with you, Jessica?"

I don't respond.

After we do our exercises and warm-ups, we break into smaller groups to practice our dances for the spring show. The daffodils head for the front part of the room, near the door. Tiara Girl and her spring-thunderstorm pals stay in the center. We robins head toward the back. We've only learned a little of our dance so far, so there's not much we can do until Mr. Lester, who is helping the daffodils right now, makes his way back to us. "But that's silly," I hear a daffodil girl tell him. "How can a daffodil jump?"

Mr. Lester closes his eyes. It looks like he and the girl have been through this before. "You're not actually *being* daffodils," he says. "You're embodying the spirit of daffodils. You'll jump with joy because it's spring, and you can finally come out of your bulb in the ground. And you'll spin around as you feel the sun on your new leaves."

"But I don't get it," the girl persists. "How can a daffodil spin? Its roots would get all tangled up."

Mr. Lester looks as if he'd like to yank this particular daffodil out of the garden and put in a nice, quiet rock instead.

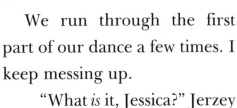

We run through the first part of our dance a few times. I keep messing up.

"What *is* it, Jessica?" Jerzey Mae asks, her eyes full of concern. My friends and sisters gather around me.

Well, I'm going to have to tell them sometime. "I brought Adrienne to school. I thought I *had* to," I say, before they can interrupt me. "Rose and Mason were both home. And when I went to talk to Ms. Debbé, the cat got out of my dance bag and a man saw it, and now Ms. Debbé is going to lose her lease and the school has to close because there can't be animals in the building." I choke back a sob.

No one moves. Then Epatha says, "That was a crazy thing to do, Jessica. What were you thinking?"

72

"The school is really going to close?" Jerzey Mae asks.

"Why didn't you just put the cat in your closet or something?" asks Al.

"Or tell Rose not to go in your room and to keep Mason out?" asks Brenda. "You could have said you had a science experiment set up or something." I'm glad she's not talking backward, because I'm too upset to translate.

"I don't know," I almost shout. "I had to do something fast, and I just couldn't think of anything else. I was worried about Adrienne."

"Well, now we've got to worry about Adrienne *and* Ms. Debbé," says JoAnn.

Suddenly I get mad. We've all been through a lot together. When Brenda borrowed those special toe shoes from Ms. Debbé's office and her cousin's dog ate them, I didn't tell Brenda she was crazy. When Al couldn't learn her dance solo by herself, I didn't yell at her. "I thought you were my friends," I say. Then

I walk to the side of the room, pick up my dance bag, and head for the door.

Mr. Lester asks where I'm going. "I feel sick," I say. "I'm going to wait downstairs."

I tell the school secretary I don't feel well, which is an understatement. She asks if she should call my mom; I say no.

I sit on a cold, hard bench in the waiting room, all alone. I've never been in this room by myself.

There's only twenty minutes till the class is over, but it's the longest twenty minutes of my life. My stomach feels as if it's full of rumbling rocks. My face feels hot. No ballet school. No home for Adrienne. And all my friends hate me now. Everything's a total mess. I am starting to feel actually sick, not just pretend sick.

Feet pound on the stairs. Class must finally be over.

My friends and sisters come up to the bench together.

"Jessica—" Terrel begins.

"Lo sentimos," Epatha says, interrupting her. "We're sorry."

"We were just taken off guard," Al says.

"You've always stuck by us when things were tough," Brenda says.

"Plus, you're our sister," Jerzey Mae adds.

"You're our Sugar Plum Sister," Terrel says, correcting her. "And Sugar Plum Sisters stick together." A look of fierce determination comes over her face. "And we'll figure out a way to help Adrienne. *And* Ms. Debbé," she says.

The knot in my stomach eases, at least a little. "But how?" I ask.

JoAnn tilts her head. "Well, since our mom happens to be a lawyer, she might be a good place to start."

Chapter 10

We decide that we'll talk to our mom that afternoon. "But we absolutely can't mention Adrienne," I warn my sisters.

"Duh," JoAnn says. Jerzey Mae nods vigorously.

The other Sugar Plums will call their school friends and ask if anyone wants a cat. Suddenly things don't seem so hopeless after all. As Jerzey Mae, Jessica, and I walk off with Mom, I turn around. Terrel gives me a thumbs-up.

We wait till we get home to tell Mom about the ballet school situation. First, I take Adrienne back up to my room, where she scampers under the bed. Clearly, she's had enough traveling for one day. After I give her some fresh water and wet food, I go back downstairs.

Mom's settled in the living room with a cup of tea and a book. JoAnn is sprawled on one end of the couch, and Jerzey Mae sits primly on the other. I sit in the easy chair, which seems wrong, since I feel very uneasy.

"Hey, Mom," JoAnn says casually. "What if a landlord wanted to tear down a building and put up condos? Could he kick out the people who are renting the building?"

Mom looks up from her book. "It depends. Real-estate law is complicated. If they have a lease, he might have a hard time kicking them out."

"What if they broke the lease somehow?" Jerzey Mae asks.

Mistake. One of us casually asking about something might have slipped under the wire, but two of us asking is definitely going to trigger Mom's alarm system.

"What's this about?" Mom asks, suspiciously.

JoAnn looks at me as if asking whether or not we should just spill the beans. I'm thinking we can spill some of them, but not all.

"I heard Ms. Debbé and some man talking in her office today," I tell Mom. "He wants to tear down the Nutcracker School so he can build condos. And Ms. Debbé's lease may have been broken," I add, not mentioning that it was broken by the cat I'm not even supposed to have.

"How was the lease broken?" Mom asks.

Jerzey Mae opens her mouth, but JoAnn nudges her hard with her foot, indicating to her that she should keep quiet.

"I don't know," I lie. I've lied so much in the past two days that I wouldn't be surprised if my nose started to grow like Pinocchio's. But if I tell Mom about Adrienne, she might make us take her to any old shelter, and they might put her to sleep. I figure it's okay to fib if it saves the kitten's life.

Mom considers this. "Well, a broken lease makes things more difficult. But sometimes buildings can't be torn down if there's something special about them. For instance," she says, "some buildings are considered historic. You can't just tear those down. If the man can't tear the building down, maybe he'll lose interest."

"How can you tell if a building is historic?" I ask, trying to keep the excitement out of my voice. The Nutcracker School building sure *seems* old. Maybe there's a way out, after all.

"Hmmm . . ." Mom pauses to think. "There are historic-building registries. Tell you what," she says. "One of my friends from law school works for the city. I'll give him a call and see what he can find out." She looks around at us. "But are you sure you heard right, Jessica? It seems to me that if the school were in danger,

Ms. Debbé would have said something to the parents. Maybe you misunderstood."

I'm sure, all right. And it's confirmed the next day, when Mom comes into the kitchen with the printout of an e-mail from Ms. Debbé.

"Well," Mom sighs, "this says that due to circumstances beyond Ms. Debbé's control, the school will be closing. And that your final dance performance has been moved up from April to March twenty-fifth—just two weeks away—so she hopes all the girls will practice extra-hard to get their dances learned by then." Mom folds the e-mail up. "I'm sorry, girls. But I'm sure we can find another place for you to take ballet."

JoAnn slouches in her chair. Jerzey Mae stirs her cereal listlessly.

"It wouldn't be the same," I mumble.

"Why is the school closing?" Mason asks.

Mom explains about the lease stuff, while I stare at my orange juice. I think about what Ms. Debbé told me—that Mr. Evans would have found some reason to close the school even if Adrienne hadn't jumped out of my bag—but it doesn't make me feel any better.

"Did you hear back from your friend yet?" I ask. "The lawyer friend?"

"Not yet, sweetie," Mom says. She puts her hand on my arm. "But please don't get your hopes up, Jessica. From the sound of Ms. Debbé's e-mail, it may already be too late to help."

I spend as much time as I can in my room with Adrienne. She's getting much bolder, and her paw is almost healed. She can walk on it just fine, and she's even gaining weight. When I pet her, instead of feeling her ribs sticking out, I feel a little round tummy. She likes playing with the cat toy Terrel brought over and chasing a bottle cap across the room. But she still won't sit on my lap.

Wednesday night, while I'm playing bottle-cap hockey with Adrienne, the door flies open.

"Hey! You got a cat?" Mason says, dropping to his knees to pet Adrienne.

I run to slam the door shut. "Mason, you know you're supposed to knock!" I say.

He ignores me. "How did you get it? I thought Dad was allergic."

"She's not an *it*; she's a *she*," I say. "And Dad doesn't know. Neither does Mom."

Mason runs his hands along Adrienne's back. He's much more gentle than I would have expected. Adrienne freezes in alarm, then seems to decide Mason's okay. She lets him pet her for a few minutes, then begins to wash her face with her paw.

"She's so cute!" Mason exclaims as he scratches Adrienne's head. "What are you going to do with her?"

I shake my head. "I don't know." Looking at him severely, I add, "But you *cannot* tell Mom, okay? She might make us get rid of Adrienne right  away, and I want to find her a good home first."

"Of course I won't tell. Wow, Jessica," he says, looking at me in admiration. "I think this is the first bad thing you've ever done!"

"Well, I'm not happy about it," I reply. "I just didn't know what else to do. I couldn't leave her out on the street with a hurt paw."

We sit in silence as Mason continues to stroke Adrienne. "I think she's purring!" he says.

"She likes you."

"I wish we could keep her."

"Not a chance." I sigh.

"Can I come in and visit her sometimes?" Mason asks.

I think about this. If I say no, he might get mad and tell Mom. "Okay," I finally say. "But you have to *promise* not to tell anyone. And *promise* to make sure the door is closed very tightly when you come and go."

Mason turns out to be surprisingly helpful. The next day, when Mom comes up the stairs, he starts talking really loudly so that I'll have time to hide Adrienne. He even uses his allowance money to buy her three cans of a special kind of cat food.

"Tyrone's cat likes this kind best," he says. He opens up a can and watches as Adrienne devours the contents. "See? I knew she'd like it," he says, pleased with himself. "Don't worry, Adrienne. We're going to find you a really great place to live. Aren't we, Jessica?" He looks at me with his huge brown eyes.

"Sure we are," I say. I just wish I knew how.

By Thursday night, I've heard back from the other Sugar Plums. None of their friends wants a cat. Correction: a lot of their friends want a cat, but their parents won't let them have one.

JoAnn continues to call shelters in the hopes of finding someplace that can take Adrienne sooner, even after the rest of us give up. "I found one in New Jersey that will take her," she reports.

"New Jersey? How would we get her to New Jersey?" Jerzey Mae says.

"Dunno," JoAnn says bleakly. "But at least it's something."

Mom doesn't hear back from her friend until Friday. I'm busy feeding Shakespeare when she knocks on my door.

Quickly I scoop Adrienne up and put her under the bed, where she likes to hide. Only then do I open my door a crack.

"I heard back about the Nutcracker building," she says. I can tell from the look on her face that the news is not good. "The building is pretty old, but it's not considered historic. That means it's not protected."

I stand very still taking in the news. I guess that's it, then. There's no hope.

"I'm sorry, baby," Mom says. "I know how much the school means to you. To all of you," she adds as Jerzey Mae and JoAnn join her in the hallway.

"Well . . . thanks for trying," I tell her.

"I do have some good news for you girls, though," Mom says. "Your dad's coming home earlier than we expected."

"When?" we all ask together.

Mom smiles. "Tomorrow!"

Chapter 11

Mom doesn't get quite the response she probably expected.

"*Tomorrow?*" JoAnn repeats. "You've gotta be kidding."

Jerzey Mae's mouth drops open in horror. "That's two whole weeks early! Why?"

"One of his students got pretty sick, and your father didn't want him traveling home alone," Mom says. "The other professor is staying in Africa with the other students."

"What time tomorrow?" I ask.

"I'm going to pick him up while you're at ballet." Mom looks at each of us suspiciously. "What's going on? Aren't you happy he's coming home early?"

Jerzey Mae bails us out. "We're making him a welcome-home card," she says breathlessly.

I jump in. "Yes, and now I guess we'll just have to do it faster than we thought. Right, JoAnn?"

"Yeah," JoAnn says. "Fast."

Mom relaxes. "Well, that's lovely, girls. I'm sure he'll appreciate it." She heads downstairs. "Dinner in fifteen minutes," she calls back to us over her shoulder.

Jerzey Mae and JoAnn join me in my room. We close the door tightly. Adrienne jumps out from under the bed and pounces on JoAnn's untied sneaker laces.

"*Now* what are we going to do?" JoAnn asks. She slumps onto the floor and waves one shoelace around to give Adrienne a moving target.

"Well . . ." I say weakly, "maybe Adrienne can still stay here. Maybe Dad's not *that* allergic—"

"Oh, yes, he is," Jerzey Mae says. "He picked me up at Anita's house once, and she has a cat. Dad was sneezing like crazy the minute he stepped in the doorway."

There goes that idea.

Adrienne loses interest in the shoelace. Jerzey Mae, who's sitting on the floor next to JoAnn, picks Adrienne up and puts her on her lap. Adrienne crawls off immediately, but then curls up on the floor beside her.

"We're going to have to tell Mom," JoAnn says after a long silence.

"No, we are not," I say.

JoAnn exhales loudly. "Then what are we going to do? You can't take the cat to ballet again, you know."

I don't respond.

She looks at me and her eyes widen. "Oh, no. Jessica, tell me you're not planning to take the cat to ballet again. Are you crazy? After all the trouble that caused the first time?"

"I guess you're right," I say. "That would be pretty stupid."

I *don't* say that I'm not going to do it, however.

"How many more days till we can take her to Cat Crazy, anyway?" JoAnn asks.

Jerzey Mae looks at the calendar on my wall. "Still more than two weeks."

JoAnn stands up. "You're just going to have to hide Adrienne in your room and hope Dad has a head cold or something that keeps him from smelling her."

"Maybe we can spray perfume all over the house," Jerzey Mae suggests.

I shake my head. "I don't think that's going to do it, Jerz," I say.

They leave me alone with Adrienne. I pet her tummy as she sprawls out on the floor beside me. Finally, she falls asleep. She snores cute, delicate snores. Every once in a while her back leg twitches, as if she were dreaming about chasing a mouse (or a giant shoelace). I gently stroke her, careful not to wake her up.

What if Dad does find her when we're gone? Will he drop her off at some bad shelter before we get home from ballet?

I can't take that chance.

Chapter 12

So, the next day before dance class, I put Adrienne back into her shoe box and back into my dance bag. Other than getting her out of the house, I have no plan. None. Maybe I can beg one of the other Sugar Plums to hide her for a week. Maybe I can ask one of the other girls in ballet class to take her. All I know is that this will keep her safe for another few hours.

JoAnn and Jerzey Mae meet me in the hallway outside our rooms. "Did you hide Adrienne?" JoAnn asks.

"Yup," I respond. I'm not going to tell my sisters what's going on, partly because I don't want JoAnn yelling at me, and partly because I don't want them to get into trouble, too.

JoAnn looks relieved. "Good," she says. She pats my shoulder, which surprises me—she's not a touchy-feely person. "Don't worry, Jessica. Maybe Dad's not really *that* allergic."

"Ha!" Jerzey Mae says.

"Well, maybe Dad's plane will be late," JoAnn says, glaring at Jerzey Mae. "He's coming all the way from Africa—"

"It's on time," Jerzey Mae says gloomily. "I checked the flight number on the computer."

JoAnn seems to be out of pep-talk material. "Let's go," she says. "It'll probably be okay." But then she looks back at my doorway with concern.

Epatha and Amarah walk us to class, since Mom's already left for the airport. I lag behind as we crunch through the newly fallen snow. "She's worried about the cat," JoAnn whispers to Epatha, just loudly enough for me to hear.

She's got that right. Adrienne isn't just sitting still this time the way she did before.

The top of my dance bag is popping up and down as she paws at the fabric. Even though it's freezing, I take off my scarf and drape it over my bag. When we go up to the dance studio, I don't leave the bag in the waiting room as I usually would. Instead, I bring it along, set it on the floor, and prop my coat against it, hoping that will hide Adrienne's movements.

Class seems to last forever. As we plié, I ask the girls on either side of me if they want a cat, like, now. One says she might, but she has to ask her mom first, and her mom's out of town. The other sounds interested until she finds out that Adrienne isn't orange. "I really want an orange cat," she says.

"But why?" I ask. "This cat is really sweet. And she's playful, too."

She shrugs. "An orange cat would look nicer in my bedroom."

"She's a living being, not a fashion accessory!" I say with vehemence.

"Ladies!" Ms. Debbé calls. "No chattering! Please concentrate. Graceful arms! Glide down. Do not pop up and down like the jeff-in-the-box."

"Like the *what*?" a new girl asks, bewildered.

"She means 'jack-in-the-box,'" JoAnn says.

Adrienne, still hidden in my bag, seems to be doing her own ballet. As we practice at the barre, I look on with horror as my coat slips down off the bag, which then creeps slowly toward the middle of the dance floor.

"To the center of the room, girls!" Ms. Debbé calls. "Grand jetés!"

Thank goodness. This gives me a chance to race over and shove the bag back against the wall before I get in line. I keep watching out of the corner of my eye, but the bag has settled down. Maybe Adrienne has gone to sleep.

After our jetés, we break into groups to practice our dances for the performance—the

final performance at the Nutcracker School of Ballet, Ms. Debbé reminds us. Today, she's dressed in stark black, and she looks ten years older than last week. But she still stands tall, her head high and her body perfectly erect.

We work on our robin dance. Usually, I would be thrilled about dancing with my friends, especially in an animal dance. But I'm too worried about Adrienne to enjoy it. This

may be the first time in history that a robin has worried about keeping a cat alive.

Ms. Debbé comes to watch us. "Left leg more straight, Alexandrea! Yes . . . and Brenda, graceful arms. Arms like wings." We soar in a circle, then gracefully duck down as though we're hunting for food. For a brief moment, I become a robin, swept away by the music and the movement.

Until I almost trip on my dance bag, which has edged toward us again.

I look around to see if anyone's noticed. Fortunately, the girls in the other groups are still working on their dances. Terrel, Brenda, Al, Jerzey Mae, and Epatha are busy concentrating on their steps. But JoAnn sees the bag. She stops dancing for a moment and stares at me in disbelief. I swoop down, robinlike, and carry the bag to the side of the room.

"Very interesting, Jessica, but that is not part of the dance," Ms. Debbé says. "Robins are not, how do you say, carrier pigeons. Robins, they do not carry luggage."

"Sorry." I dash back to the dance floor.

JoAnn continues to give me the evil eye. I ignore her and flap, flap, flap my "wings."

Finally, Ms. Debbé claps her hands, signaling that class is over. "Very good work, my dear ladies. You will all be brilliant. Two more weeks," she says. "Practice while you are at home. Practice, practice. This will be a very good show. The best ever."

She leaves. The other girls pack up and trickle out of the room.

My stomach twists. Class is over. Dad will be home soon. And I still have no idea what to do with Adrienne.

"Jessica, can I use your lip balm?" Al asks.

"Sure," I say, distracted. I look at the clock and try to figure out how long it will take Dad to get home from the airport. He'll have to go through customs, since he's coming back from another country. That could take a while.

"*Aaaaaah!*" Al yells.

I turn to see a black-and-white blur racing past my friends' feet and out the door of the studio. Al is standing next to my dance bag, a look of horror on her face.

Chapter 13

"I didn't know Adrienne was in there!" Al says.

Oh, no. My lip balm was in my dance bag.

How many stupid things can I do in my life? Because I think I've already done my share for the next twenty years.

"Get moving!" Terrel hollers.

We race into the hallway and frantically look around. No sign of Adrienne, but there are several rooms with open doors.

"Triplets, upstairs!" Terrel barks like an army commander. "Al and Brenda, downstairs! Epatha and I will take this floor."

JoAnn, Jerzey Mae, and I race up the wooden stairs as the other Sugar Plum Sisters fan out to cover their assigned territories.

"What's on this floor?" Jerzey Mae asks breathlessly. "I've never been up here before."

"I was once," JoAnn says. She's ahead of us even with her weak leg. "I helped Mr. Lester put some costumes in storage."

Sure enough, the costume storage room is on our left as we reach the top, but the door's closed, so Adrienne can't be in there. We peer into the dusty room beside it, but it's empty.

JoAnn goes back into the hallway and looks around. "I don't see where she could possibly be," she says. "She must have gone downstairs."

"You guys!" Jerzey Mae shouts. She's at the far end of the hallway.

Almost hidden in an alcove is a narrow flight of wooden stairs. "It must be an attic or something," says JoAnn.

"Do you think it's safe?" Jerzey Mae asks.

The stairs do look a little rickety. They're steep, and the stairway is dark.

"Sure," I say, even though I'm not.

I gingerly place one foot on the first step. It creaks, but feels stable. So up we go, though there's a squeak after every step. I'm first, JoAnn's next, and Jerzey Mae brings up the rear.

We emerge in what is indeed an attic. The floor is covered with dust. A few cardboard boxes are scattered around on the floor, and wooden beams reach from floor to ceiling. I thought it would be dark up here, but sunlight streams in from a row of windows along the front of the building. We head toward the light.

There, perched on a window seat, is Adrienne.

"Phew," JoAnn says. We hurry toward the cat, who doesn't even seem to notice us. She's fixated on something just outside the window. We join her and look out.

The attic window looks out over part of the

roof, where a large gray bird with a curved beak and light feathers on her underside is keeping watch. A small brown egg rests at her feet. The bird doesn't seem to notice her feline observer, but she probably wouldn't be too worried even if she did, because she's about ten times bigger than Adrienne.

"Wow," JoAnn breathes.

"What a beautiful bird!" says Jerzey Mae.

Adrienne turns and glares at us, as if we were talking during a movie, then goes back to eyeing the bird.

The bird looks familiar. I close my eyes and try to picture the birds in my bird book. I get a tingly, excited feeling, as if it's really important that I figure this out.

Then all of a sudden I know.

And I know why it might be important.

"Get the others and meet me in the office," I say. "Hurry!"

Chapter 14

The secretary of the ballet school is surprised when we all show up in the reception area begging to use the Internet on her computer, but she lets us. And in just a few clicks, I've confirmed what I thought.

"The bird's a peregrine falcon," I say.

My friends don't respond.

"Hey!" I say. "Did you hear me?"

Al says, "Yeah, so? What's a paraffin falcon, or whatever?"

I'm practically bouncing up and down now. "They're really rare! And just let me check one more thing." I lean over the keyboard and check a few Web sites while my friends impatiently hover behind me.

Suddenly, there it is, right on the screen—exactly what I'm looking for.

"Yes!" I say triumphantly. "They're a protected species."

Jerzey Mae leans forward to look. "What does that mean?"

"It means you can't hurt the birds or their eggs. I think tearing down the building where the birds nest would hurt them, don't you?"

"So, this might help us save the building?" Brenda asks.

"You bet it might," I say, scooping Adrienne up and dropping her back into the dance bag. "Come on. We need to tell Ms. Debbé." We dash out, leaving the secretary blinking in confusion.

Ms. Debbé is sitting at her desk staring out the window. We cluster around her doorway. She doesn't notice us, but she looks up when I gently tap on the door.

"Hello, girls," she says, sounding startled. She motions all of us in to her office, and we gather around her desk.

"Ms. Debbé, there's a peregrine falcon nesting on the roof," I say. "They're protected birds. I don't think the building can be torn down if there are protected birds living here."

Ms. Debbé sits very still. "You are sure it is really a peregrine falcon?" she asks.

"Yes," I say firmly.

Ms. Debbé sits up straighter than usual. "A protected bird—surely they couldn't tear down the building," she says, almost to herself. Her eyes light up with hope, but then she seems deflated again. "I'm afraid Mr. Evans will just wait until the chicks leave, yes? Then there would be no reason to keep their nesting place safe."

My friends and I exchange looks. She has a point.

Ms. Debbé leans back in her chair. "It was

a good idea, girls. And I am grateful you, too, want to save the Nutcracker School."

"Just let me think," I say. It's as if there's some missing piece of the puzzle that I'm just not seeing.

Ms. Debbé smiles sadly. "I think perhaps you should not worry about saving the school. It is a very big job for young ladies, and even I cannot figure out how." She pauses. "However, you had a kitten you wanted to keep here for a time. Is this still true?"

Surprised, I nod.

"Fine," she says. "If they are making us leave the building anyway, a little more of this, how do you say, lease-breaking will not do any harm. The kitten may stay in the attic, at least until the school closes. It will be nice to have a little company when I'm here alone," she adds. "I have always been rather fond of cats."

"Oh, *thank* you, Ms. Debbé," I say. My legs feel like spaghetti. I nearly sink to the floor in relief, but JoAnn catches me. That will be enough time for us to get Adrienne into Cat Crazy. She'll be safe. No one will put her to sleep or hurt her. I feel tears well up in the corners of my eyes.

"When would you like to bring her here?" Ms. Debbé asks.

The cat, actually, is three inches away from Ms. Debbé's feet, trying to poke her paw through my bag. "Uh . . ."

Terrel interrupts: "We'll bring her up in ten minutes. Come on, guys," she says, pulling on my arm. I grab my bag, and we follow her out of the office.

Terrel scans the waiting room. "Amarah's picking us all up, right?" she asks Epatha.

Epatha nods; we were all going to hang out at Bella Italia till our mom and dad got home from the airport.

"Call her and tell her to stop first at the pet store on the corner and get some litter and a litter box and some food, okay?" Terrel says.

Epatha does this. And a few minutes later, Amarah comes through the front door of the school.

"I don't even want to know," she says, handing Terrel the cat supplies. "This is me not asking."

We race back up the stairs.

"Here's the kitty," I say, presenting the bag to Ms. Debbé.

"A dance bag?" Ms. Debbé asks. "Is that how you carry cats?"

"Sometimes," I reply honestly.

Ms. Debbé unzips the bag and pulls out Adrienne, who is now squirming up a storm. She holds the cat up to her face. "Hello, my dear," she says. "Aren't you the beautiful one?"

Adrienne sniffs Ms. Debbé, then rubs her head against Ms. Debbé's face. She seems perfectly happy to be held by Ms. Debbé while she is standing. But as soon as Ms. Debbé sits down in her chair and tries to put Adrienne on her lap, the cat jumps down to the floor.

"She's not really a lap cat," Epatha explains, grabbing Adrienne before she can dart out the door.

Ms. Debbé smiles. "She is lovely. What is her name?"

I gulp. We all look at each other. I don't know if Ms. Debbé will be mad or flattered to know I named the kitten after her.

"I named her Adrienne," I say. "Because she's elegant, and she reminds me of you." I leave out the part about the white mark on the cat's head looking like a turban, just in case Ms. Debbé wouldn't like that.

Ms. Debbé's face is strangely still. It almost looks as if she's going to cry. But she simply nods and says, "Thank you, Jessica. I am honored to have such a lovely cat for a namesake."

Phew. I've made a lot of bad decisions lately. I'm glad I made at least one good one, too.

Chapter 15

My friends and I take Adrienne, up to the attic. I can't believe the kitten is safe—and that she has all the cat stuff she'll need for a while.

"That was amazing, you guys," I say to Terrel and Epatha. "Thanks for calling Amarah!"

Epatha smiles broadly. "*No hay problema—*no problem."

Terrel glares at her. "It was my idea."

Epatha tosses her hair. "It was *my* sister."

"Fine," Terrel says under her breath. She rips open the bag of cat litter and pours it into the litter box they've brought. Al and Brenda head off to get water for Adrienne, and Jerzey Mae puts some dry food into a bowl.

As we get the kitty settled in, Ms. Debbé

comes upstairs. We show her the falcon. "Such a shame to take this place away from these lovely birds," Ms. Debbé says. "When I was little, there was a nest in our front tree. The birds came back year after year to the very same spot."

I sit bolt upright. "That's it!" I say.

Everyone looks at me. "What's it?" Al asks.

"Don't you get it?" I ask. "Even if the birds are gone, it doesn't mean the falcons won't come back. They use the same nesting sites every year."

Brenda nods. "Oh, yeah! I remember reading about some hawk's nest on a co-op building. People took it down after it was empty." She closes her eyes as if she's a computer pulling up a document she'd saved a long time ago. "It wasn't illegal, but everyone got really mad at the people who did it. They got a lot of bad press."

"What's bad press?" asks Jerzey Mae.

"She means people said bad stuff about them," I reply quickly. "And people definitely don't want bad press. I'll bet Mr. Evans doesn't want bad press."

Ms. Debbé tilts her head, puzzled. "But how will anyone know about the falcons' nest?" she asks.

Terrel's eyes glow with determination. "Oh, they'll know," she says. "Just wait and see."

"So, Terrel—how *will* anyone know about the falcons' nest?" I ask.

Since Mom and Dad aren't home yet, Amarah's dropped us all off at Bella Italia, as planned. We're sitting at our favorite table eating tasty garlic bread. We each have a glass of soda—all except for Brenda, who's been reading up on dental problems, since she wants to go to medical school. "Aren't you worried all that sugar will rot your teeth?" she asks us.

"Nope," Al says, taking a big slurp.

"Terrel?" I ask again.

Terrel finishes chewing her garlic bread and delicately pats her mouth with a red-and white-checked napkin. "TV," she says emphatically. "We gotta get on TV. The local news. More than one station if we can."

Brenda looks unconvinced. "Why would they put us on TV?" she asks. "We're just kids."

"Are you kidding?" Terrel responds. "That's *why* they'll put us on TV. We're kids. We're cute. We're trying to save our ballet school. News places are always looking for stories about kids or animals. This story's got both!"

She looks around at us. "We should probably dress up in pink clothes so we look cuter. Jerzey Mae, you should wear those pink ribbons in your hair. JoAnn, you'll definitely need to lose the baseball cap."

Jerzey Mae bounces with excitement.

JoAnn looks disgusted. "Do we have to?"

Terrel glares. "It's to save the Nutcracker School, JoAnn."

JoAnn sighs.

"But how do we get the TV people there?" Jerzey Mae asks.

"I haven't figured that out yet," Terrel says.

There's a silence as we all think and chew. "Animal-protection groups!" I say. "Especially bird ones. I'll bet if we call some and tell them about the falcons, they'll help us."

"We can have a protest," Al says. "My mom took me to one once. We stood around with signs and yelled. It was kind of fun."

"Perfect," Terrel says. "Next Saturday after class, we'll have a pink, frilly protest outside the ballet school. If Mr. Evans tears down the building after that, everyone in New York will hate his guts," she adds with satisfaction.

Terrel is sure this plan will work. I wish I was, too.

Chapter 16

"Look who's back!" Mom calls out when we open our front door.

Dad gives us each a big hug. "I missed my girls!" he says.

"And you missed your boy!" Mason hollers from the living room, where he's sprawled on the couch.

"And my boy," Dad says, grinning.

"We missed you too, Dad," JoAnn says. She, Jerzey Mae, and I follow him into the kitchen, where he's in the middle of eating a peanut-butter sandwich.

"I haven't had peanut butter in weeks," he says. "I missed it almost as much as I missed all of you."

JoAnn helps Mom unpack the groceries; they must have stopped at the store on the way back from the airport. "There are ten jars of peanut butter in here!" JoAnn says.

"I told you I missed it," Dad replies.

Jerzey Mae and I sit at the table with him as he attacks another sandwich. "So, what's been going on?" he asks. "Did I miss any excitement?"

JoAnn tells him about the ballet school maybe having to close. Then I tell him about the falcons.

Mom pricks up her ears, because she's interested in endangered animals. "An actual peregrine falcons' nest in Manhattan? How fascinating. Who found it?" she asks, as she pulls a box of crackers out of a grocery bag.

Jerzey Mae and JoAnn freeze.

"Um . . . Adrienne," I say.

Mom stops in her tracks. "Since when

do you refer to Ms. Debbé by her first name, young lady?" she asks.

"Sorry!" I say, neglecting to tell her that I was actually referring to a kitten. I quickly move on to telling them about how we're hoping the falcons will keep Mr. Evans from tearing down the building.

"Terrel says we need to have a protest and get on TV," Jerzey Mae says.

Mom puts down the crackers. "That's not a bad idea," she says.

Suddenly, I feel more hopeful. If Mom thinks we can do it, maybe we really can. "We're going to call up some bird protection groups and see if they can help us get the word out," I tell her.

Dad seems lost in thought. "Hmmm . . . one of my old students works in a TV newsroom. Why don't I give her a call and see if she has any ideas?"

"Great!" I say.

* * *

Mason comes into my room later looking for Adrienne. "I didn't get to say good-bye!" he wails after I tell him what happened.

"I'm really sorry, Mason," I say, and I truly am. "But I had to get her out of here before Dad got home."

Mason leaves the room, and for a minute I'm afraid he's so upset he'll go tell Mom and Dad about our having kept Adrienne here. But instead he comes back with two more cans of cat food he bought with his own money, and makes me promise to give them to Adrienne. I give him a big, relieved hug. "And I promise you'll get to say good-bye to her before we take her to the shelter," I say.

As the week goes on, I get more and more excited about the upcoming protest. Dad's ex-student says she'll do her best to get a camera crew to the ballet school at noon on Saturday. Terrel, Brenda, Al, and Epatha tell Ms. Debbé about our plan, and Ms. Debbé agrees to contact the other parents in case their kids want to be at the protest, too. I'm not counting on it, but if even a few of them show up, it'll help. Dad's TV friend says the more people there, the better.

Meanwhile, I've called some bird advocacy groups to tell them about what we're planning. One guy in particular was very excited to hear about the nesting falcons and said he'd let his members know about the protest. Another person said she'd ask a reporter she knows to try to get a story into the newspaper.

Jerzey Mae and JoAnn spend hours making signs. Jerzey Mae does the painting. She even borrows my bird book so she can make accurate pictures of the peregrine falcons. JoAnn hammers sticks together to make handles and supports for the signs; then Dad helps her attach everything with a staple gun.

"Do you think we've made enough?"

Jerzey Mae asks on Friday afternoon. There are about twenty signs scattered on her floor.

"I guess so," JoAnn says. "It might just be the seven of us, you know."

"Eight," I say. "Ms. Debbé will be there, too."

We stack up the signs. Then we select out-fits for tomorrow's event so we'll look cute, just as Terrel advised. JoAnn has absolutely nothing dainty or pink. "When was the last time you saw a skateboarder in a frilly skirt?" she grumbles. So she borrows a tutu from Jerzey Mae.

That night, I lie in bed awake for a long time. What if no one comes to the protest? What if Ms. Debbé loses the school? What if we have to find a new ballet class with a new teacher? What if none of my friends can take class together anymore?

I hear Shakespeare scrabbling around in his cage. He doesn't have to worry about anything. All he has to do is eat and sleep and play.

For just one moment, I actually wish I were a rat.

Chapter 17

My stomach is in knots as we pack up the signs on Saturday. Mom and Dad drive us to the Nutcracker School, since we have so much to carry. Jerzey Mae is dressed in a pink tutu. I'm wearing a pink leotard and a ballet skirt. I try not to stare at JoAnn in her borrowed tutu. She looks like a completely different person. If you didn't know her, you'd think she was a lovely little ballerina—until she opens her mouth.

"Stupid itchy stuff," she mutters, shifting around in the backseat. "Why would anyone in her right mind wear a skirt like this?"

We pull up to the school and unload the signs. It's hard to stay focused during class. The other girls aren't wearing anything special, so they may not be staying around for the protest afterward. I hope it's not just my friends and me.

After class ends, my friends and I stay in the classroom with Ms. Debbé. She looks nervous, too. But she clears her throat and finally speaks.

"Whatever happens, I want to thank you girls," she says. "This thing you are doing to help me, I appreciate it very much."

"It's going to work, Ms. Debbé," Terrel says.

"How much longer?" JoAnn asks.

We all look at the clock. "We should go outside in a few minutes," I say. "If the news people come, they'll come at noon, and we want to be outside when they get here."

"Why don't we head down now?" Ms. Debbé says.

We slowly walk down the stairs. The

waiting room is empty. Rats—I was hoping at least some of our classmates would stick around, but I guess they didn't.

As we pick up the signs, I hear a dull roar. It seems to be coming from outside. We exchange puzzled looks, then push through the front door. Ms. Debbé gasps.

A sea of people greets us. Our classmates *are* there—looks like every single one of them. And there are lots of grown-ups— lots and lots of them. There must be more than a hundred people gathered in front of the school. Some of them have their own signs: I see SAVE THE BIRDS!, FALCON POWER!, and BIRDS LOVE THE NUTCRACKER SCHOOL OF BALLET! Some people wear feathers or bird wings. One lady even wears a hat that looks like a falcon's head.

"Wow," I breathe. All of my friends and sisters are looking around at the crowd, dazed. None of us can believe it.

Terrel comes to her senses first. "Save the falcons!" she hollers at the top of her lungs. It's amazing someone that little can yell so loud. The people in front of the school take up the chant. *"Save the falcons! Save the falcons!"*

As if on cue, we see a graceful bird soar through the air, with some sort of small animal wriggling in his beak.

"He must be bringing food to his mate," I say.

The falcon seems totally unconcerned about all the noise below, but I guess if he's a city bird, he's used to it. As he lands on the ledge, the crowd goes wild.

Terrel quickly passes out the signs, and we begin to march around in front of the building. A moment later, two TV trucks pull up to the curb. As we chant, a skinny lady in a red blazer and lots of makeup climbs out. A woman carrying a television camera joins her.

"A TV reporter is here!" Terrel announces. "Remember, everyone—be cute. No one can resist cute little kids." She practices a big, fake smile.

"Holy cow, T.," JoAnn says. "You're scaring me."

Terrel ignores her. "Cute, cute, cute. Think cute."

The red-blazer lady fluffs up her hair, then picks up a microphone and starts talk-

ing to the camera. I see her walk over to Ms. Debbé, but I can't hear what she's saying, because everyone's yelling. Then the reporter squeezes past the rest of the crowd and stands in front of me and my friends.

"Why are you lovely girls out here today?" she asks, before shoving the microphone into my face.

"Because someone wants to tear down our ballet school," I say, before I even have a chance to get nervous. "And there are per-egrine falcons nesting on the roof. Falcons come back to their nesting sites every year. So, even after the eggs hatch, the falcons still might need the building."

The woman looks surprised. "My good-ness! You certainly seem to know a lot about birds," she says.

"She does," Terrel interrupts. She unfurls a really big smile. Anyone looking at her would think she was just an adorable little girl, not a drill sergeant. "And there's no law to protect the nesting spot after the chicks are gone, so this dude—I mean this gentleman—can tear down the building after the birds leave. Doesn't that stink?"

I know that newspeople are supposed to be impartial. They're not supposed to say who they think is right; they're just supposed to report the news. "Uh . . ." the newswoman stammers. "What would you like people to know about your ballet school?"

"We're having a special dance recital next Friday," I say. "People should come to show their support for the school and the falcons."

Terrel moves up to the microphone again. "We're even doing a special dance in tribute to the falcons," she says.

"We're going to be robins, not falcons," Brenda hisses at her, but Terrel steps on Brenda's foot and gives the camera another cheesy smile.

"Well, there you have it," the reporter says, turning back to the camera. "The struggle of a determined group of little girls to help keep a falcons' nest—and their ballet school—open for business. Back to you, Chuck."

The cameraperson fiddles with the camera, and the reporter lady turns back to us. "Good luck, girls. I hope you save your school," she says. I guess they don't have to be impartial when the camera's off.

"Thanks," I say.

We keep marching and shouting for a while longer, and then the people start to drift away. Mom and Dad, who have been watching from the sidelines, come over to us.

"Good job, girls," Dad says.

Mom nods. "We're very proud of you—all of you—for standing up for what you believe in."

"How do we know if it worked?" Brenda asks.

"No way to tell yet," Mom says. "But maybe other bird lovers will see the news and want to help."

My friends and I exchange looks. I think we'd all kind of hoped that someone would rush in with a notice from the mayor saving the building or something.

But it looks as if all we can do now is wait.

Chapter 18

"Hurry, Jessica! Get your costume on!" Jerzey Mae says. "We're supposed to be dressed by six thirty!"

It's the night of our dance show. We're in one of the classrooms at the Nutcracker School. Al's mom is helping with the costumes, as usual. Right now she's repairing a daffodil's drooping leaf. Tiara Girl, who's all in gray because she's a thunderstorm cloud, is telling Al's mom that clouds are supposed to have a lot of glittery rhinestones. Al's mom isn't buying it, however.

"Clouds don't glitter, April," she says. "Please go join the rest of your group. I've got my hands full here."

Tiara Girl stomps off. Terrel smirks.

I peek into the hall. As usual before a show, the whole Nutcracker School is in chaos. One of the beginning ballet classes is doing a cat-and-dog dance, so black-and-white Dalmatians and furry tabby cats are chasing each other all around the room. Gumdrops and licorice from another class's candy ballet are jumping up and down, and a banana is running away from a giant grape.

"Settle down!" Mr. Lester hollers. No one listens. He sighs. "Why do we do these shows again?" he says, to no one in particular. A red lollipop races past him, followed by a girl surrounded by a cloud of pink fluff—I think she's supposed to be cotton candy.

I go back to the dressing room and put on my costume. Ms. Debbé found out what Terrel told the reporter and, surprisingly, has decided that we should make some changes. So, our robin dance is now our falcon dance.

134

Al's mom wasn't thrilled about the last-minute adjustments, but somehow she still came up with some really great falcon costumes for us. Ms. Debbé spent some time up in the attic with her feline namesake, watching the falcons come and go, and added some falconlike moves to our dance.

Adrienne seems to be doing fine in her new temporary home. We've been getting to class early to play with her, and on the days that we don't have class, one or two of the Sugar Plum Sisters will stop by to feed her and clean her litter box. Mr. Lester's been helping, too. Once, I went up and found him sitting on the window seat with Adrienne curled up right next to him. "Not much of a lap cat, is she?" he remarks.

"Don't feel bad," I say. "She won't sit on anyone's lap. Not even mine." I gently scratch her under the chin, just where she likes it.

"I guess she'll be in a shelter soon," he says.

"Yup," I say. I'm trying not to think about that part. Even though she's caused a lot of trouble, it's hard to think about her ending up living with some stranger.

"I wish I could take her," Mr. Lester says. "But I'm in a no-cats building."

"I'm sure the shelter will find her a good home," I say, hoping with all my heart that I'm right.

A red gumdrop runs into me. "Sorry!" she says, before running off after a green gumdrop.

Ms. Debbé sticks her head inside the dressing room and tells us that she's decided the falcon dance will be last, even after the dances by the bigger kids.

"Wow," Epatha says. "She must think we're really good!" She admires her feathery headdress in the mirror. "Falcon power!"

Music airing in the auditorium drifts up as the show begins. All the excitement of the last week is making me even more nervous than I usually am before a performance. My friends look nervous, too.

Epatha is pacing around in circles.

Brenda is taking deep breaths. "Down you calms it," she announces to Epatha in back-ward talk. "It try should you."

Epatha just paces faster and faster.

Terrel practices some of the dance moves over in a corner, but she jumps, startled, when the sound of applause hits the room.

"That's pretty loud," she says. "Isn't that louder than usual?"

"I think so," JoAnn says. "Come on—let's sneak down and see how many people there are."

But one of the mothers guards the door. "Please stay here, and stay together, girls," she says.

Terrel rolls her eyes.

Before we know it, Mr. Lester calls us. "Okay, falcons—you're on in two minutes!"

We follow him downstairs and wait by the stage entrance.

"Ms. Debbé will tell the audience a little about the falcons; then I'll cue you to go on," Mr. Lester says. "Break a leg!" (*Break a leg* is what you say to people before they go onstage. It means "good luck.")

"No, thanks," JoAnn mutters. "I've already done that."

We hear Ms. Debbé's muffled voice, then more applause. Mr. Lester opens the door, and I lead the group onstage.

The loud clapping almost hurts my ears. It's hard to see out into the audience, because there are bright stage lights shining in our faces. But the auditorium is completely packed. Every single seat is full. People are crammed in like sardines. They're standing in the back, and rows of kids are even crunched in to the space that's between the front row and the stage.

Wow.

I see a tall man in a suit standing off to one side of the room. He looks like Mr. Evans. I wonder why he's here. He seems like the last person who would come to one of our ballet shows. But before I can think more about it, the music starts, and we begin to chassé and flap our wings.

Epatha and Terrel stand in front and do pirouettes as the rest of us jeté across the stage, spreading our wings as though we're flying. I listen to the music. Suddenly, the audience disappears and I am a falcon, soaring through the sky with my falcon friends.

After our dance is over, the audience explodes in applause. People jump to their feet. Someone starts a chant: *"Save the falcons!"* More and more people join in, until the whole room is chanting along.

I look at Terrel and grin. I don't know if we've saved the birds or the ballet school. But we've sure given it our best shot.

* * *

After the show, there's a reception downstairs. My friends and I go out and join our families.

"Great job," Dad says, hugging JoAnn, Jerzey Mae, and me at the same time.

Mom joins in the hug. "My girls, the fabulous falcons!" she says.

"Not bad!" Mason says. "For a bunch of

girls," he adds, grinning. JoAnn whacks him gently on the head.

My friends' families all tell us how much they liked the dance. "It made me want to be a falcon, too!" Epatha's dad says, flapping his arms.

"Falcons don't eat pasta, *amore mio*," Epatha's mom reminds him.

"Ah! Then never mind," he says.

A crowd surrounds Ms. Debbé. "I want to make a donation," I overhear a man saying. "You'll need money to fight this developer, and I want to help."

"Me, too," says a woman.

"My Falcon Fanciers Club will hold a bake sale," the woman who wore a falcon hat at the protest says to Ms. Debbé.

Suddenly, I'm aware of Mr. Evans, who is standing on the outer edge of the group surrounding Ms. Debbé. He clears his throat. "That won't be necessary," he says.

Everyone stops talking. "A good business-person knows when to move on to other battles," he says. "I see now that tearing down this building would be a public-relations nightmare. The Nutcracker School—and the falcons—can stay."

The cheer that rises up from the room now is the loudest yet. My friends and I jump up and down. My mom hollers. Even my dad whoops, and he is definitely not the whooping type.

Only Ms. Debbé is quiet. While the room erupts, she stands as still as a statue. Then she regally draws herself up and walks over to Mr. Evans. "Thank you," she says, extending her hand.

He takes it. "I've fought big companies and won," he says. "But I guess I'm no match for seven determined little girls."

Ms. Debbé smiles. "Don't feel too bad," she says. "These are very special little girls."

After the reception, we all change back into our regular clothes.

"Good work, Sugar Plums," Terrel says. "Another mission successfully accomplished." She zips up her bag with a flourish.

JoAnn shakes her head. "I can't believe it," she says. "The school is safe."

"And so are our feathered friends," says

Epatha. "Those falcons have style."

Al pulls on her socks. "When you think about it, it's pretty weird that a cat ended up saving a bunch of birds," she says.

"Jessica!" Jerzey Mae says in alarm. "You fed her before the show, right?"

"Yes, Jerzey Mae," I say. "She's fine." I take a deep breath. "But you all know that we take her to Cat Crazy tomorrow, right?"

Everyone stops moving. "Already?" Brenda says. "Man." She looks down.

"I'm going to miss her," says Jerzey Mae.

"Me, too," Al says. She looks miserable.

"I hope they find a good home for her," Epatha sighs. *Una casa buona.*

We sit in silence for a minute. "I think we should go say good night to her," I finally say. There's a lump in my throat, and I feel as if I might start crying.

"Yeah!" Epatha says. "Let's go!"

"Just a sec," I say, remembering that I'd

promised Mason a few days ago that he could say good-bye to Adrienne. I pull him away from the cookies at the reception; then we all race up to the attic together.

"That's weird," Al says as we go up the stairs. "Why is the light on?"

We reach the top of the stairs. And there, on the window seat, is Mr. Evans.

Adrienne is sitting in his lap, purring so loudly we can hear her from across the room.

Chapter 19

We all freeze in our tracks. "Unbelievable," Al says.

Mr. Evans looks up. "Hi, girls," he says. "I just thought I'd come up and see the birds who saved your building. And this little kitten found me."

We don't say anything.

He pets Adrienne's back. Even though his hands are big, he's gentle with her.

"She looks familiar," he says. "Might this be the cat that escaped from your bag?" he asks me.

I nod. "We named her Adrienne." I'm not sure why I tell him this, but he laughs.

"With the little turban on her head," he says. "Clever."

Adrienne pushes her head against Mr. Evans's hand.

"She's never sat on anyone's lap for that long," I say.

"Despite the fact that you probably think I'm a monster, I'm not," he says. "I'm not so crazy about falcons that keep me from making a lot of money, but I've always liked cats. My own cat, Amanda, died three months and one day ago."

The fact that he says *three months and one day* tells me everything I need to know. Anyone who knows exactly how long ago their cat died must really have loved that cat.

"Would you like to have Adrienne?" I ask.

My friends turn and stare at me.

The man looks up. "Isn't she yours?"

I shake my head. "I found her, but I can't keep her. We're going to take her to a shelter tomorrow."

Adrienne stands up in Mr. Evans's lap,

walks around in a circle, then settles back down. "But I think she'd rather be with you," I add.

Mason goes over and pets Adrienne on the head. She nuzzles him, but clearly she's not moving out of Mr. Evans's lap. "I think she wants to be with you, too," Mason says.

Mr. Evans scratches Adrienne's ears. He seems to be considering this. "All right," he says. "I can't build my condos. But I get a cat. Seems like a fair trade to me."

Adrienne mews in agreement.

Chapter 20

We all go downstairs together. Ms. Debbé is surprised that Mr. Evans wants to keep Adrienne. Mom and Dad are surprised to find out that there was a cat living in the ballet studio. Mr. Lester is surprised that Mom and Dad didn't know about the cat. Before Mom and Dad get any more surprises—such as finding out that the cat was living in our house for a while—Terrel announces, "I think we should all go out for pizza!"

"*¡Sí!*" Epatha says. She looks at Mr. Evans. "You want to come?"

He shakes his head. "I have a lot to do. I'm getting a new family member soon, you know." He pulls on his jacket and wraps a scarf around his neck. "I'll come by tomorrow to pick up the cat—if that's okay with you."

"That is fine," Ms. Debbé says, "with both Adriennes."

Before Mr Evans. leaves, he tells us we can come visit Adrienne whenever we want. This is the icing on the cake.

"Thank you again, girls," Ms. Debbé says. "Without you—I do not know what would have happened."

And then maybe the most surprising thing of all happens. Ms. Debbé, who is definitely not the *huggy* type, hugs each of us, one right after the other.

* * *

When we get outside, it's as if all the excitement and worry that have been bottled up inside me need to get out. "Race you!" I say to the other Sugar Plums, and I zoom to the end of the block. My friends follow, yelling and screaming.

We stop at the corner and catch our breath, laughing. That's when I see the dog.

He's big and brown, with black markings. He comes straight over to me, sniffs my leg, then lies down at my feet.

"How cute!" I say. "But he's not wearing a collar. I hope he's not lost." I look around for his owner, but I don't see anybody.

"Oh, no, no, no," JoAnn says. "Not again!"

"Jessica," Jerzey Mae says, tugging at my sleeve. "You can't keep a dog in your room! You just can't!"

Just then, a man whistles, and the dog jumps up. "Sorry if he was disturbing you," he says. "He wants to go home with everyone. Come on, Buddy!"

The dog obediently trots off behind the man and disappears into the night.

"Thank goodness," JoAnn breathes.

I'm relieved. Really, really relieved.

And really, really ready for pizza. "Last one to Bella Italia has to wear a tiara!" I yell. And my friends and I speed off into the night, with our parents racing to keep up with us.

Jessica's Guide to Ballet Terms

barre—a railing at the side of the ballet studio that you hold on to when you're doing warm-up exercises, such as pliés. It's a nice word, because it's easy to rhyme: *To be a ballerina star, you need to practice at the barre.* See?

châiné turns—quick turns that move you across the room, unless you're not concentrating because you're worried about something. Then they're quick turns that stop when you crash into another dancer—for example, Terrel.

dance bag—bag in which you carry your ballet slippers and other ballet supplies. Can also be used as a cat carrier if absolutely necessary, which it sometimes is, no matter what JoAnn says.

grand—means *big*, so a grand jeté is a big leap, and a grand plié is a big knee bend. And grand trouble is what you might get into if you take a kitten to ballet class.

jeté—leap. Adrienne is very good at these, especially if she's aiming for your toes while you're lying in bed.

peregrine falcon—type of bird that sometimes nests on buildings. Falcons don't have much to do with dance, unless they're living on top of your ballet school.

pirouette—a spin done on one leg. Our family has a no-pirouetting-in-the-kitchen rule now, because Mason kept spinning into

Mom and Dad while they were trying to make dinner.

plié—knee bend. Can be useful if you need to search under Dumpsters for stray kittens.

Shakespeare—one of the greatest playwrights and poets ever. There are ballets based on some of his plays. Shakespeare also happens to be the name of a lovely pet rat.

tendu—a move where you stretch your foot out to the front, back, or side without letting it leave the floor. Tendus are difficult to focus on when your dance bag is creeping into the center of the room because there's a cat in it.